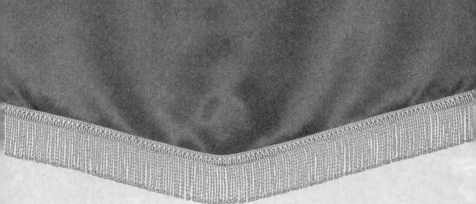

The Alliance

Gabriel Goodman

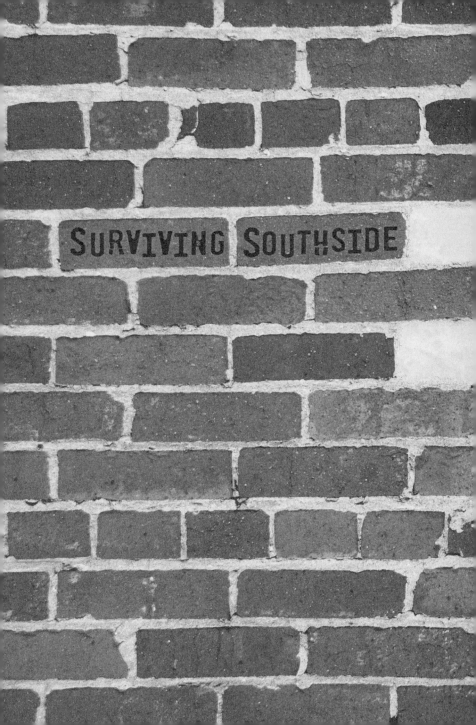

SURVIVING SOUTHSIDE

The Alliance

Gabriel Goodman

MINNEAPOLIS

Darby Creek
A division of Lerner Publishing Group, Inc.
241 First Avenue North
Minneapolis, MN 55401 U.S.A.

Website address: www.lernerbooks.com

The images in this book are used with the permission of:
© iStockphoto.com/Cliff Parnell,(main image) front cover;
© iStockphoto.com/Jill Fromer, (banner background) front cover and throughout interior; © iStockphoto.com/Naphtalina, (brick wall background) front cover and throughout interior.

Main body text set in Janson Text LT Std 55 Roman 12/17.5.
Typeface provided by Adobe Systems.

Library of Congress Cataloging-in-Publication Data

Goodman, Gabriel.
        The alliance / by Gabriel Goodman.
            pages   cm. — (Surviving Southside)
        ISBN 978–1–4677–0595–0 (lib. bdg. : alk. paper)
        [1. Gay-straight alliances in schools—Fiction. 2. High
    schools—Fiction. 3. Schools—Fiction.] I. Title.
    PZ7.G61366Al 2013
    [Fic]—dc23   2012032139

Manufactured in the United States of America
1 – BP – 12/31/12

This book is
dedicated to All
who fight
for equality.
—G.G.

CHAPTER 1

SCOTT

The *Houston Chronicle* buried the story about Jamie Ballard in section B, page 8, the same day Mr. and Mrs. Ballard buried Jamie.

I sat at the memorial, glad to see the room was full. Glad to see I wasn't the only one who cared. It was only three weeks into senior year, and hardly anybody at school had said anything about Jamie. I only overheard, "Ya hear about Jamie Ballard? Little faggot went and killed himself."

"You need a new suit," Cory said, tugging at the collar wrapped tight around my throat. "You're gonna suffocate."

She was right. The suit barely fit. I'd packed on a lot of muscle over the summer, training hard to make sure I was a starter my last year on the football team. When I heard about Jamie, getting a new suit had been the furthest thing from my mind. All I could think about was how Mrs. Ballard sounded when she called to tell me. I'll never forget that voice. Like it had been shredded with razors.

I couldn't stop looking at Jamie's mom and dad sitting up by the closed casket. Jamie's senior picture was in a frame on a table between them. Mr. Ballard tried hard to smile and thank people for coming. Mrs. Ballard . . . She could hardly do anything. She just sat there, limp, sobbing without making a sound.

I felt Cory's cool fingers lace with mine. Tearing my eyes away from Mrs. Ballard, I smiled at Cory. "Thanks for coming with me. Missing a day of school and all."

She wrinkled her nose and played with the tiny cross that hung from her neck. "I'm here for you, Scott Joshua King. You remember that."

"I know you and Jamie weren't exactly friends . . ."

"He meant a lot to you," she said, squeezing my hand and smiling, "and you mean a lot to me. It doesn't matter if Jamie and I were friends. You're hurting, and if I can help, *that's* what matters."

I pulled her close and kissed her on the forehead. Cory *had* always been there for me, ever since we started dating a year ago. She was so good to me.

Jamie and I used to hang out on the roof of his house, watching stars. I would tell him how great Cory was. Sometimes I think he got jealous. But Jamie and I had been best friends since kindergarten. He knew we were buds, no matter who I dated.

As people wove around the funeral home, I eavesdropped on Jamie's family members sharing stories about him. In some stories he was a bratty kid. In others he was an angel.

Every story was absolutely true. Jamie was all those things. But the one thing nobody in the room mentioned: Jamie was also gay.

Sometimes I tried to imagine what it was like to be him. When he came out to his parents, they told him they still loved him. The rest of his family, though, wasn't that nice. He used to tell me about the nasty looks he got from aunts and uncles at family gatherings when they thought he wasn't looking. He didn't care. "They'll miss me when I'm gone," he used to say.

I wondered if that was a sign. That I should have seen he was thinking about killing himself. It hurt my head to think about it. But he was right. The family who had whispered about him like he was some dirty secret sure missed him now. Mainly because they were pretending he'd never come out.

Jamie didn't deserve relatives like that. Nobody does.

Pastor Jacobs, who'd known Jamie since he was born, said really nice things about Jamie and urged us all to hold him in our hearts. I stood at the back of the room, a lump in my throat. Cory rubbed my back. I'd promised myself I'd hold it together. But by the time Pastor Jacobs was done, I don't think anyone could stop crying.

Things started breaking up as people filed out to head to the cemetery. I was just about to leave when Mr. Ballard touched my shoulder.

"Scott," Mr. Ballard said, "would you help my wife to the car?"

"Yes, sir," I said. Mrs. Ballard could barely stand on her own. I took one hand, and Cory took the other. We walked her slowly out to the Lincoln Town Car parked right behind the hearse. She never said a word, not even when Cory said how sorry she was about Jamie and that she was praying for the Ballards.

I looked back at the door of the funeral home. The funeral director and his assistants were bringing the casket through to load it into the hearse. Mr. Ballard stood in the entry, talking to a sheriff's deputy. He reached into his pocket and handed the deputy something shiny. Even from that distance, I knew what it was: Jamie's cell phone. It was hard to miss in its silver sparkle case. The deputy tipped his hat and walked away.

I handed Cory my keys. "Can you start the car? I'll be right there."

When Cory went to start the car, I intercepted Mr. Ballard. "Everything okay, sir? I noticed the deputy."

Mr. Ballard looked at his wife, then pulled me aside like he wanted to make sure she didn't hear. "The police are investigating. Jamie was being bullied. He got threatening text messages, people harassed him on Twitter. They're trying to figure out who it was."

He gave me a pat on the back, then got into his car. I stood there for a second, numb. No way was Jamie being bullied. I would know. He was my best friend. He would have told me, and I would have straightened it out.

But Mr. Ballard wouldn't have contacted the police if he didn't have some evidence. I felt my stomach knot up. Jamie had been hiding this from me. We told each other everything. How could he not tell me?

I walked back to my car to find Cory in the passenger seat, smearing gloss on her lips. "You okay?" she asked as I slid into the driver's seat.

No. I wasn't. My best friend was dead. Bullied to death. And I hadn't known anything about it. My knuckles went white as I squeezed the steering wheel. As the funeral procession pulled away from the parking lot on its way to the cemetery, I fell in line. But I was hardly paying attention the entire drive there. Jamie's face kept appearing no matter where I looked.

I couldn't let his death be for nothing. Jamie had always been there for me. No matter what I did or how stupid I acted, he defended me to anyone. I couldn't just let this pass. I had to find out who was giving him a hard time. And more important, I had to make sure this didn't happen to anybody else at school.

But how?

CHAPTER 2

CARMEN

"**¡D***ios mío!*"

I decided a long time ago that hearing Ma utter that every morning when she saw how I'd dressed was pretty much like her saying, "I love you, my precious daughter." Kind of.

I stood at the stove, making my famous huevos rancheros for breakfast. She'd barely set foot in the kitchen before her eyes raked over me. It was hard to tell what was offending her fashion sense this time. The baggy pants. The holes in the baggy pants. The combat boots. The sleeveless shirt. The henna tattoos up and down my arms. She clicked her tongue. Same routine every day.

To finish off, she narrowed her eyes and gave a long, hard look at the lip ring. Always the lip ring. It probably bothered her more than my entire wardrobe combined.

"You are the daughter of two very successful attorneys," Ma said, pouring us each a cup of coffee. "People are going to think we don't buy you real clothes." She, of course, had on her beige power suit, ready for another day in court.

"I am the daughter of two very successful attorneys who spend every working minute fighting for the rights and freedoms of the little guy," I said, teasing her with a smile. "That means me."

My parents were way too cool to tell me how to dress or how many piercings I could or couldn't have. But that didn't mean they had to like my choices in either department. And if good-natured sparring with Ma every morning was the price I had to pay not to wear dresses, so be it.

"I swear I won't do anything to soil the name of the House Mendoza," I said dramatically, throwing the back of my hand to my forehead. Ma grumbled. I could tell she was regretting sending me to Shakespeare Summer Camp two years ago.

Ma took plates from the cupboard and started setting the table. "You were out late last night. You and Sara go to the movies?"

I turned my back and smothered the eggs in an extra portion of black beans. I didn't have the heart to tell her that Sara and I broke up at the beginning of the summer. My parents liked her a lot. She was my first serious girlfriend. We'd been together a year. Right now, I didn't feel like explaining the whys and hows of the breakup. So, if she thought I was at a movie with Sara, I'd let her believe that. It beat explaining that I'd been hanging out at Loco Cacao, sipping lattes with Ricky and bemoaning the fact that I was single again.

"Sorry," I said. "Movie ran later than I thought."

"Just so long as you don't make it a habit," she said. "Senior year's not the time to let your grades slip."

I saluted her with my spatula. It was three weeks into the school year. They hadn't even started assigning *real* homework yet. Besides, my transcripts had already gone out to all the colleges I was interested in. A slip in my senior-year grades wasn't going to matter much.

Papa walked in, staring at the morning edition of the *Houston Chronicle* on his iPad. He kissed my cheek, goosed Ma, and poured orange juice for everyone. "*Chica*," he said to me, "did you know this boy at school? The one who committed suicide?" He tapped the iPad.

I shrugged. "Not really. I knew who he was. He got picked on a lot."

Papa nodded. "So it would seem." He tilted the screen so I could read it. The headline read: POLICE INVESTIGATE

SOUTHSIDE HIGH SUICIDE AS HATE CRIME.

It made me wanna hurl. *Of course* it was a hate crime. You had to be blind not to see how often that Jamie kid was getting shoved in the hall and taunted. Last year I'd chased off a couple guys who had backed him into a corner. Probably a dumb move on my part. I'm sure he never heard the end of it, getting saved by a girl. But I couldn't just let them do it. I kept thinking, *That could be me.* And I know I'd want somebody to have my back if that was the case.

"I wonder if his parents have a lawyer," Ma mused, scanning the article. She put her hand on Papa's arm. I smiled. They couldn't resist doing a pro bono case when they smelled injustice. God, I love my parents.

"You see this sort of thing a lot?" Papa asked.

I served eggs to everyone. "Every day."

I said it without thinking. It was true. But suddenly, Ma and Papa got *that* look in their eyes. That concerned look.

"To you?" Ma asked as I joined them at the table.

I waved it off. "Sometimes. Nothing physical. Just name-calling. I give as good as I get. But that's me."

"Do you feel safe at school?" Papa asked.

"I guess," I said. "But I've got a lot of friends who've got my back. Not everybody who gets bullied has friends like mine."

"Why don't the teachers do anything?"

"They do. Sometimes. But a lot of what happens, they never see. It's in the halls, after school, online."

Ma tsked. "No one should have to put up with that."

As we ate breakfast, I kept sneaking glances at the story on Papa's iPad. I caught words like "death threats" and "intimidation." Wow. Jamie Ballard had it worse than I thought. I knew all about the intimidation. I heard the names he was called. But I never knew someone had threatened to kill him.

You hear that kind of trash talk in the halls all the time: "I'm gonna kill you, man." But you never take it seriously. If the police were looking into it, Jamie must have been getting worse than some tough-*hombre* words shouted at him between classes. And it must have been bad enough to make him take his own life.

Ma must have seen me deep in thought. She reached across the table and took my hand. "Promise me, Carmen, that if anyone threatens you like that, you'll tell us."

"Sure, yeah, I promise."

I said it because I knew that's what she wanted to hear. But really, I was thinking, *Anyone who threatens me better be ready to back it up, because I don't take that crap from no one.*

Even so, a small part of me couldn't stop looking at the article on the iPad and thinking, *Am I really safe?*

CHAPTER 3

SCOTT

"**A** what?"

Ren and I were the last two in the showers after football practice. He was doing that thing he always did, sticking his head under the water and pretending he couldn't hear me.

I threw my shampoo bottle at him. "It's called a GSA, jerkwad. It stands for Gay–Straight Alliance. I was reading about them online. It's a group where gay and straight students can get together."

Ren shut off the water and grabbed his towel. "Sounds lame to me."

"It's not lame. It's so gay kids can feel safe." I followed him into the locker room, towel around my waist. The rest of the team was finishing up getting dressed. This was my first year on varsity. Jon Renquist was the only guy I knew well. We weren't exactly close, but we'd come up from JV together. I figured he might understand my idea. Guess I was wrong.

"Safe?" he asked, flicking the dial on his locker's combination lock. "Like, from ninjas?"

I snapped him with my towel. "Would you be serious? I want to start one here at Southside. I think it's important."

"But you're a dude, right? I mean, you don't like other dudes. Or are you trying to tell me something?"

I rolled my eyes. "That's why it's a Gay–*Straight* Alliance. You don't have to be gay to join."

"But why would a straight guy wanna join?

All the fags would just sit there and think about doing it with you. Gross."

I was about to tell him not to use the word *fag*, but I figured why bother? Morons like Ren would never figure it out. "In your dreams, Renquist. Not every gay guy wants to have sex with you. Besides, the group's not about that. It's about finding ways to fight homophobia."

Ren shook his head. "Whatever, man. Let somebody else do this. You shouldn't be the one starting it."

"Why?"

"Think about it. People will think you're into dudes. *I* just thought you were into dudes."

Not everyone's as dumb as you, Ren, I thought. But I said, "Everybody knows I'm dating Cory Walton."

"So? God, they'll think you're bi or something. That's even worse."

I clenched my teeth and tried not to blow up. This was exactly why our school needed a GSA. To educate people. To fight this kind of ignorance. Getting mad at Ren wasn't going to help.

"There's nothing wrong with being gay," I told him calmly. "A GSA would make people understand that."

Ren pulled on his high-tops and laced them up. "Why do you care all of a sudden? I never heard you standing up for the fairies before. When did you go all soft?"

"Jamie Ballard was my best friend. I don't want what happened to him to happen to anyone else."

Ren snorted. "Little queer killed himself. You can't stop that kind of thing."

Seriously, you needed the patience of a saint to have a conversation with Ren. "Mr. Ballard told me Jamie was being bullied. Somebody harassed him until he couldn't take it anymore. Threatened his life, even. You're wrong. That kind of thing *can* be stopped. And it *should* be stopped."

Ren got quiet. He looked around to see if anybody else on the team was listening, then leaned in.

"Dude, don't you have enough to do already? You're already in, like, six clubs already. You've got football now, baseball in the spring. You're on track to be valedictorian. You go starting a new club, you won't have time to study. You'll blow it all ... why? Just because some perverts are getting picked on? Not worth it, dude."

Ren punched me on the shoulder before grabbing his backpack and leaving. I don't know why I bothered trying to talk to him about it. At least it showed me that I had a lot of work ahead of me. And there was one bright spot: trying to explain it to the rest of the school could never be as hard as trying to explain it to Jon Renquist.

＿＿ ＿＿ ＿＿ ＿＿ ＿＿

Cory met me outside the locker room. She threw me a toothy smile and handed me a mango smoothie, like she did every day after practice.

"You're the best," I said. I downed half the cup immediately.

Cory linked her arm with mine, and we walked down the halls. "Are you feeling better?"

"Not really. I can't stop thinking about Jamie."

"Would you like to come with me to church on Sunday? You could talk to Father Erikson. I always talk to him when I'm sad or confused."

I didn't want to offend her, but religion was never really my thing. "Thanks, but that's okay. I was doing some research online last night, and I think I know one thing that might make me feel better. Do you think the office is still open?"

"I doubt it. School got out an hour ago. Why?"

"I need to get the paperwork to start a new club."

Cory's eyes lit up. "Oh, that sounds fun. What kind of club?"

I explained to her about the GSA I wanted to start in Jamie's memory. She smiled and nodded.

"That'll be a lot of work," she said. "Are you sure you'll have time for it? What about your grades?"

Ugh. Something was wrong with the world when my girlfriend was asking the same questions as Ren.

"I'll *make* time for it. This is really important to me. I feel like I should have been there for Jamie. I feel like I let him down."

Cory drew me close and kissed me hard. She pulled back slowly so that only our foreheads were touching. She looked me right in the eye.

"I bet you anything that if you could ask him, Jamie would say you never let him down. I'm sorry that, for whatever reason, he didn't think he could tell you about everything that was going on. But it wasn't your fault. You were such a good friend to him."

I really wanted to believe that. Some nights, I stared at the ceiling and got mad at Jamie. It seemed so selfish for him to kill himself and not even give me the chance to help him. But then I turned it around and got mad at whoever made him feel like his life wasn't worth anything. Like suicide was the only way out. I didn't know what I'd do if I ever found out who did that to him.

"Let's go," I said. "I can stop by the office in the morning. First thing tomorrow, we lay the groundwork for Southside's new GSA."

Cory's lips pulled back. It looked like she was smiling, but I couldn't really tell. If I didn't know better, I'd have thought she was biting her tongue.

"Sure," she said. "Tomorrow."

CHAPTER 4

CARMEN

I couldn't help it. I laughed out loud. Mr. Olson gave me his dirtiest look ever. And he'd given me plenty since school started. From the minute I walked into his class, his looks told me exactly what he thought of me. When Ma looked at my clothes, she just hated that they weren't her style. When Olson looked at me, his eyes said, *Troublemaker*.

Olson turned back to the whiteboard to

continue explaining the themes in *The Scarlet Letter*. I looked down at the note Ricky passed that made me laugh in the first place.

NO JOKE. SCOTT KING IZ STARTING A GSA.

Scott King? The football player? He was a complete and total tool. Oh, sure, he wasn't your typical dumb jock. He got good grades. But he was such a . . . *golden boy*. A lily-white, self-centered jerk that all the teachers adored. What did he care about the queer students in school?

I scribbled on Ricky's paper. PROBLY SOMETHING FOR HIS COLLEGE RESUME. HE'LL GET BORED N SAY WELL HE TRIED. SOME IVY WILL LET HIM IN JUST FOR TRYING.

Ricky snatched the paper, read my note, and nodded with a grin.

When the bell rang, everybody gathered up their stuff. Ricky and I were headed for the door together when Mr. Olson blocked us.

"Miss Mendoza," he said, folding his arms. "I hope this isn't going to be a problem *every* class."

I wanted to tell him off so bad. Three weeks I sat there and listened to him drone on every day and never once did anything wrong. Except that laugh. One stupid laugh, and now I'm the class scuzzball.

"No, sir," I said, thinking how much I'd like to sic my parents on him for singling me out. But I liked to fight my own battles. I was giving Olson this round. But if I kept my nose clean and he kept coming at me, we were going to have a problem.

Ricky and I slipped into the hall and joined the river of students. "Why does he have it in for you?" Ricky asked.

"Because I'm not *normal*," I said, batting my eyes and flouncing like a beauty pageant contestant. "Some people are so threatened by anyone not exactly like them. But I'm playing it cool. I'm not giving him anything to nail me on the rest of the semester. I'll wet my pants before I ask for a bathroom pass, I'll hold a sneeze all hour. But he ain't getting nothing on me."

We bumped fists and made our way down to the first floor for Mrs. Carney's Intro to

Film History class. Everywhere we went, people said hi, high-fived us. We were like a power couple, only we weren't dating. Ricky was single. I didn't know for sure if he was gay or not. He'd never dated anyone, and he never wanted to talk about it. So I just let him be.

Mrs. Carney was standing by the door when we strolled in. Unlike Olson, Mrs. Carney was cool. She never played favorites. If you were being a jerk, she called you out, but then she didn't hold it against you. And where Olson just droned on and on about a book he *clearly* couldn't care less about, Mrs. Carney loved what she taught.

"Good morning, Ricky, Carmen," she said just as the bell rang.

We took our seats in the back corner as Mrs. Carney dimmed the lights. "We'll continue our unit on Alfred Hitchcock," she said, turning on the TV at the front of the room, "by watching *Psycho*."

"Ree! Ree! Ree!" Ricky shrieked, doing his best impression of the *Psycho* theme. This chick in front of us jumped. Everybody laughed, including Mrs. Carney. Once the movie started, things got quiet.

About half an hour in, Ricky leaned over and said, "Is it just me, or does that Norman Bates guy look like an older version of Scott King?"

I choked back my laugh, having gotten in trouble once already for that. But he was right. Norman Bates wasn't as buff as Scott King, but they both had those clean-cut, all-American-boy looks. The resemblance was only creepier knowing what Norman Bates does in the movie.

I still couldn't believe he was trying to start a GSA.

"But, you know," I said to Ricky, "it's not a bad idea."

"What?"

"The GSA. That Jamie Ballard kid got bullied to death. We need a group here where the queer kids can go to feel safe and supported."

"So, why don't *you* start the group?" he asked.

"No comments from the peanut gallery," Mrs. Carney called out from her desk. That's what she said to shut people up during the movie. I had no idea what a peanut gallery is.

Yeah. Why didn't *I* start a GSA? There was no way Scott King was going to see it through. He'd do just enough so it looked good on his college applications and then walk away. Meanwhile, a *real* GSA could be doing *real* work.

I spent the rest of the class daydreaming what our GSA would do. By the time the bell rang, I'd had the whole alliance built, staffed, and working hard. This was gonna be awesome.

━ ━ ━ ━ ━

I ran to my locker after film class. I had a lot of plans to make to get the GSA up and running. As I got closer to my locker, I spotted Jon Renquist coming down the hall at me. He had a dopey grin on his face, which was pretty much what I'd come to expect from him. Ren wasn't known for deep thought.

As we passed, he brushed against me, knocking my books to the floor. "Watch where you're going, douchebag!" I yelled after him. I thought I heard him chuckle as he moved on without looking back.

I scooped up by books and opened my locker. A piece of paper, slipped in through the vent, fluttered to the ground. I opened and read it.

It was Jamie Ballard's obituary from the paper. Someone had written over his picture: ONE DOWN . . . YOU'RE NEXT, TURBO DYKE.

CHAPTER 5

SCOTT

I hung out at the edge of the cafeteria as lunch started. People filed through the hot lunch line and took their seats. I clutched the clipboard in my hand and suddenly felt nervous. I got a first in the state speech and debate competition last year, but now I was having trouble working up the nerve to talk to my classmates. I decided it would be best just to work on a couple people at a time. So

I scanned the room and found a couple girls hanging out by the Coke machine.

"Hey," I said, walking up to them. "Shelly, right?"

Shelly Markham and her friend looked at each other like I'd just said I was from Mars. "Uh, yeah?" she said.

"I'm Scott King."

Again, they looked at each other. "Yeah, Scott, we know who you are." They turned away and went back to buying their drinks.

I leaned against the machine. "So, I was hoping you guys could help me out. You know what a GSA is?"

They didn't even look at me. They grabbed their Cokes and walked to the cafeteria tables. I followed and kept going.

"It's a Gay–Straight Alliance. I'm trying to start one here at Southside. Rules say I have to get at least thirty students to express interest in an organization before the school will okay it. You don't have to join. You just have to agree that there's a need for it."

Shelly and her friend sat at the edge of a

table and popped open their cans. They still weren't looking at me.

"So . . ." I held out the clipboard and smiled my best smile. "Any chance you guys would sign this to say we need a GSA?"

Finally, Shelly rolled her eyes my direction. She stared at the petition on my clipboard. She looked disgusted. "So, GSAs protect gay kids from bullies, right?"

I nodded. "Yes. But you don't have to be gay to join. Anyone can—"

"Well, who protects the rest of us from you, Scott?" Shelly's friend asked.

I blinked. "What?"

Shelly's friend shook her head. "You don't even remember me, do you, Scott? Maggie Foster? I think you called me Fattie Foster every day during junior high."

My stomach fell. Yes, I remembered Maggie. Today, she looked nothing like she did four years ago. I also remembered teasing her. More than that, I remember Jamie calling me out the summer between junior high and high school.

"Dude," he said, "lay off Maggie Foster. Your best friend is gay. I'm the easiest target at school. How would you feel if people were calling me names?"

And people *were* calling him names. And worse. But he never told me.

I didn't say a word to Maggie after that, and when we came to Southside, we hardly saw each other. Jamie had told me to apologize. I never did.

"Look," I said, "I'm really sorry about that. Really. I don't do that anymore. I'm trying to start this GSA because of Jamie Ballard. He was being bullied and—"

Shelly stood, and Maggie followed. "Come on, Maggie," she said. "We're not falling for any doglist." And they walked off.

Doglists. The football team was famous for the prank. Some guys would go around, trying to get girls to sign a petition that they claimed was to extend lunch hour or have shorter classes or some idea that was never gonna happen. Once a bunch of girls signed, they posted the list all over the school. But at the

top, it said, "WE THE UNDERSIGNED
ARE THE UGLIEST DOGS AT
SOUTHSIDE."

I felt like crap. I didn't think I'd ever done
anything to Shelly. But she probably hated me
just for how I'd treated Maggie. God, I was
stupid.

I took the clipboard and made the rounds
to all the tables. The student council, the chess
club, the Future Farmers of America. They
all sat together and all refused to even look at
the petition. I even hung out by the kitchen
window, trying to snag people as they dropped
off their trays. But nobody signed.

I wasn't going to give up. This was just one
lunch period of three. I was sure Mr. Winston,
the vice principal, would give me a pass to
miss a couple classes and try to recruit from
other periods. But I clearly needed to work on
my pitch.

"Problem, Scott?"

I looked up and found Mrs. Carney, the
media arts teacher, smiling at me. I'd had her
for Media Studies last year. She was pretty cool.

"Hey, Mrs. Carney," I said. "Yeah, big problem. I need to get thirty students to sign this, saying they think the school needs a GSA. But I'm not having much luck."

Mrs. Carney looked over the petition. "Is this about Jamie Ballard?"

"Yes, ma'am."

She nodded. "Well, you can start by signing it *yourself.* That might help. Someone needs to set a good example for the rest of the students."

I laughed. "You're right." And I threw my name down.

"What about your teammates? Football? Baseball?"

I thought about Ren. Even if I explained that signing the petition didn't mean he had to join the GSA, I don't think he'd get it. And I wasn't sure about the rest of the teams either.

"I could try," I said. "To be honest, I thought I could get a ton of people to sign. I thought . . . people liked me. I mean, not sports people. But, I guess I used to be kind of a jerk."

Mrs. Carney folded her arms and smiled.

"The good news, Scott, is that jerks can change. Everybody can change. But I don't think you have time to wait for that. So maybe you should concentrate on your strengths for now."

"My strengths?"

"You are liked, Scott. Think about it." She tapped the clipboard and walked away. Mrs. Carney was always doing stuff like that. She had an answer, but she wanted me to come up with it on my own. It was kind of annoying.

The bell rang, ending lunch. I joined everyone as they left the cafeteria and moved towards their next classes. I was almost to English when a pair of arms wrapped around my waist and pulled me aside. I turned to find Cory, grinning.

"Just wanted to wish you luck on your English test today," she said, kissing me on the cheek.

"Thanks," I said. "But what I need is luck getting people to sign this."

She looked over the petition. She didn't stop smiling, but her eyes narrowed. "Oh. You're going through with this."

"Yeah, I told you I was. I gotta get thirty students to sign it, and so far I've got one. Me."

Cory handed me the clipboard. "Jesus started with five loaves of bread and two fish, and He fed the multitudes. I'm sure you can do it."

The headache I'd started to get during lunch faded. I loved it when Cory believed in me. "Hey, since I got you here, would you sign . . . ?"

The next bell rang and she ran off. "Gonna be late for lunch!" she said. "Catch me later."

I waved as she disappeared around the corner. I wished we had the same lunch period. With her at my side, I bet I could have gotten more than thirty signatures.

I took my seat in English and waited for Mr. Olson to pass out the exam. But my head wasn't there. I needed twenty-nine more signatures. Mrs. Carney thought there was a way to do it. I just needed to figure it out.

CHAPTER 6

CARMEN

You'd think that with all the time I spent in the vice principal's office, I was some kind of public menace. At least, that's what most of the faculty thought. I never got why the stuff I did to end up in the office was considered "making trouble." I had opinions, and sometimes I expressed them. Very loudly.

I was never disrespectful. But if Mr. Olson said we couldn't read *The Adventures of Huckleberry Finn* because it contained the N-word, I would explain that the book was a product of its time and was antislavery in many ways. I expressed lots of opinions like that about the books we could and couldn't read. And sometimes, instead of having an intelligent conversation about it, the teacher would get upset at the girl with the pierced lip and send her to the vice principal.

So, it was really weird to be in Mr. Winston's office without having done a thing. I just got a note when I went to homeroom: PLEASE REPORT TO MR. WINSTON'S OFFICE. I thought maybe it was because I'd laughed in Olson's class. But as much as Olson hated me, I knew he wouldn't send me here for something like that.

"Am I in trouble?" I asked.

Winston had invited me to sit across from him at the desk but then hadn't said anything. He just sat there.

"Ms. Mendoza," he said, "I'm told you recently asked for paperwork to start a Gay–Straight Alliance in school. Is that true?"

Oh. *That.*

"Yes, Mr. Winston. It's my understanding that any student can petition to have a special-interest group started at school, provided they follow procedure. And that's what I'm doing."

Winston nodded. "And you really think there's enough interest here? I mean, I don't know any other gay students apart from you."

I bit my tongue. He was baiting me. Practically challenging me to lose my temper. No way would I give him the satisfaction.

"I'm out and proud, Mr. Winston. Sure, everyone knows I'm queer. Just like everybody knew Jamie Ballard was queer. And look what happened to him."

Suddenly, the baiter became the baitee. Winston's face flushed, and he shook his finger at me. "Nothing has proven that Jamie Ballard was bullied. I won't have you spreading rumors . . ."

"I'm not spreading anything, Mr. Winston," I interrupted him gently. "But kids are being bullied, and it's happening whether they're gay or not. You can get bullied in this school if people even *think* you're gay. A GSA would send the message that being queer is okay. It would tell queer students that they're accepted. And it would tell straight students who are accused of being gay that they shouldn't be ashamed."

Winston stewed. He couldn't do much more. I wasn't speaking loudly, just firmly. I looked him right in the eye and was careful not to look angry. He couldn't do anything to me, and he knew it.

He leaned back in his chair. "You are aware," he said slowly, "that in addition to having thirty student signatures, you also need three staff members to approve of the new organization. And one of those must agree to be the faculty advisor."

I nodded. "I read the rules very carefully, sir. I don't think it will be a problem."

Winston raised an eyebrow. He looked amused. "Oh, you don't? Ms. Mendoza, when a student goes through the proper channels to form a new school-sponsored organization, the group becomes eligible for funding. That's why we have such stringent requirements for starting a club. We can't fund any group that is poorly organized or doesn't have substantial support."

He took a manila folder from his desk and opened it up. "Any faculty member who signs the petition is putting their reputation on the line. Signing that document is the same thing as saying, 'I believe Carmen Mendoza has the ability to create and run this organization.' But I think you'll have trouble finding someone to express *that* much faith in you. A few comments from your most recent report cards . . ." He squinted at what was inside the folder. "'Carmen's grades are fine, but she shows little ability to follow through . . .' And 'Carmen has to be encouraged to complete projects on time . . .'"

Winston closed the folder, put his fingers together like a steeple, and lifted them to his chin. "Now . . . do you really think you have the faculty's confidence? It seems to me, Ms. Mendoza, that maybe you should be focusing your energy on learning to follow through on your current commitments instead of taking on a new project that, all signs are, you won't be able to complete."

My ears burned. A hundred Spanish curse words danced on the tip of my tongue. It was all I could do not to lay into him. He sat there, so smug. It was his pretending like he was only thinking of my well-being that really ticked me off.

I thought about showing him the death threat I found in my locker. It was still in the bottom of my messenger bag. Even though I'd promised to tell my parents if anything like that happened, I'd kept quiet. It was just one note. Probably someone trying to freak me out.

But I would have loved to see how Winston would react to it. I'd been shoved, taunted, called names, and bullied in just about every way you can think. This was the first time someone had threatened my life. That was something he *couldn't* ignore.

But, no. He'd only accuse me of making it up. Which only made me angrier. He could call me a troublemaker all he wanted. I'd own that.

But no one calls me a liar. If I gave him that chance, I'd say things I could never take back.

"I guess we'll just have to see, Mr. Winston," I said, doing my best to smile. I probably looked sick. "May I go now?"

He dismissed me with a nod. It wasn't until I'd walked down the hall and around the corner that I began spitting out all the curse words I'd been holding in.

He was wrong. I'd get *more* than three teachers to sign the petition. The teachers weren't dumb. They knew this kind of bullying had to stop. If I had to, I'd get every teacher at Southside to sign it.

Game on, Winston.

CHAPTER 7

SCOTT

I decided that what Mrs. Carney was trying to tell me was that I just had to suck it up and ask the football team to sign. It made sense. They were some of the most popular guys in school. If they signed, a bunch of other people would sign too. And I was their teammate. We had each other's backs. Even if I could just get a couple of them to sign, it was all I needed to get more to fall in line.

After practice, I finished showering before everyone else so I could run back and get dressed. By the time the rest of the team came from the showers, I was ready for them. As they toweled off and started dressing, I stood up on a bench and held my clipboard over my head.

"Yo, guys!" I shouted over their jabbering. Everybody looked at me and quieted down. "Hey, good practice today. I know I'm new to varsity, but I really need your help. I want to start a new organization at school and I need you guys to sign this petition to get the ball rolling."

A couple guys shrugged and stepped forward, reaching for my pen. But Ren stood up.

"Wait a sec," he said. "Is this that fag group you were talking about?"

The guys who'd approached me suddenly backed off.

"It's not a fag group," I said. I explained what the GSA was. "Everybody in this school looks up to the football team. You guys are heroes. If we take the lead and get this group started—"

"No way, man," Phil Oliver, the quarterback, said. "Don't want nobody thinking I'm queer."

"I told you, signing this doesn't say you're queer or anything . . ."

But I was sunk. Where the quarterback went, everybody went. One by one, they turned their backs. Some guys made comments about not wanting me to watch them dress. As I slammed my locker shut and stormed out, I heard someone say, "Oooh, look, boys. Mary's upset!"

Their laughter disappeared behind the door as I marched into the hall. I almost knocked Cory over.

"Whoa, Tiger," she said, jumping out of my way. She smiled and offered me a mango smoothie.

"No, thanks," I said, seething. She looked hurt and pulled it back. "I'm sorry, Cory. It's not you. I just . . . Why can't I find anyone to sign this petition?"

She put her arm around my shoulders. "Honey, you've been working on this awfully hard. But I think this is a sign that maybe you should just forget about it. You can't start a club if no one wants to join."

I shook my head. "I'm not giving up. I'll get Mr. Winston to give me permission to drop by the other lunch periods. I'll—"

She squeezed my shoulder. "It's great to see you so fired up, but I think you could be spending this energy doing something else. Something better."

I exhaled. "Something better? Cory, I'm doing this for Jamie. I owe it to him to see that the crap that happened to him stops. Look, can you just sign this?" I held out the clipboard.

Cory recoiled from it like I was holding out a spider. "Scott, I can't do that. Jamie was a sweet guy. But he made his choice. Signing that is like saying I agree with that choice."

I felt ice fill my chest. I looked at Cory as if I'd never seen her before. There she was: soft brown hair, smiling like always. But something was different.

"Choice?" I asked. "Cory . . . Do you think Jamie *chose* to be gay?"

Her fingers went to the cross at her throat. "Being gay isn't natural, Scott. It's not part of God's plan."

I stepped away from her. "You're kidding, right? Why would anybody choose to be harassed like Jamie was? Why would someone choose to be teased and shoved and threatened? How did that benefit him in any way?"

"I don't know," she said quietly. "But then, I don't know why people choose to kill. I don't know why people choose to cheat on their spouses. I don't know why people choose to defy the Lord's commandments every single day. I don't judge. That's for God to do. All sin is matter of choice, Scott, and Jamie chose to sin."

"Jamie didn't choose to be gay," I spat. "But *you're* choosing to hate him because he was."

She shook her head. "I don't hate Jamie. My church teaches us to hate the sin, love the sinner."

"Yeah," I said. "That's still hate. I thought Jesus was all about love. Or maybe you didn't read that far in your Bible."

For the first time, Cory frowned. "Don't take that tone with me, Scott King. I have a right to express my opinion. You're always cranky after practice. Drink your smoothie and you'll feel better."

But she was wrong. How could I feel better, knowing she believed this? "Sorry, Cory." I said.

She laid her hand on my arm and started smiling again. "We don't have to agree on everything. We're each allowed to have our own opinions. This is just something we'll have to agree to disagree on."

That was her solution. Agree to disagree. Like disagreeing that Blake Shelton was a better singer than Kenny Chesney. Or that burgers were better than chicken. But it didn't work like that.

"No, Cory, we can't do that. Because if we agree to disagree, you get to walk away and continue hating and people are still being bullied. And you're a part of that."

I handed her back the smoothie, took my clipboard, and walked away.

CHAPTER 8

CARMEN

I sat in the computer lab, glaring so hard at the petition that I thought it might actually catch fire. Right at the top, where the spaces for the three faculty members to sign sat. Even if every student in the building signed, the whole petition was worthless without those three signatures.

Ricky slid into the chair next to me. "You have got this, like, *death look* on your face. You must really hate that paper."

I laughed. Leave it to asexual Ricky to snap me out of my funk. "I *do* hate this paper. And I hate what people think of me. And I hate that what people think of me is wrong. I'm just Hater McHaterson today."

"Well, Ms. McHaterson, let's see what we can do about that. Nothing can be that bad. What's up?"

"I asked all my teachers today if they would sign off on the GSA. Five teachers, five nos. Not just nos. Each no was served with my very own are-you-crazy look." I pushed the petition away from me. "Winston was right. The teachers here hate me."

Ricky rubbed my shoulders. "You just asked the wrong teachers. There are *tons* of teachers you can ask. You can't give up because *five* people said no. Nobody hates you."

I snorted. "Nobody hates me? Check this out."

I got out my phone and called up my Twitter account. Most of my feed was me talking to my friends about school, homework, and movies. I scrolled down to yesterday and pointed to a tweet from someone named @VictorEE. It said:

@CMendoza No 1 will cry at you're funearl, dyke.

"I don't know what offends me more," I said. "The wrong use of 'you're' or that the idiot can't spell *funeral*."

Ricky leaned in. "Carmen, that's like a death threat."

I shook my head. "No, *this* is a death threat." I reached into my messenger bag and showed him the clipping of Jamie Ballard's obituary.

Ricky's eyes got wide. "You've got to tell someone."

"Whoever it is just wants to get in my head. That's what they did to Jamie Ballard. Well, they won't do it to me. If I tell someone, word will get around and they'll know they got to me."

Ricky didn't look convinced, but he let it go. "You said you talked to five teachers. You've got six."

I nodded. "Haven't asked Carney yet. I've been putting it off. She's awesome, and if she says no, it might really be over."

He glanced at his watch. "Well, you're in luck," he said. "Film class is next. You're going to ask her to sign, she's going to say yes, and the world will be a happy place again. Right?" He gathered his stuff and made for the door.

My phone vibrated as another tweet from VictorEE appeared in my feed.

@CMendoza heard your starting a gsa don't even try it

I stared at it a long time, wanting to ignore it. Responding would just give him satisfaction but . . .

I just couldn't back down. I couldn't. I typed:

@VictorEE Who's going to stop me? A dickless nobody like you?

I logged off and the message disappeared. "Wait up!" I called after Ricky. I felt my phone vibrate in my pocket. Probably VictorEE getting back to me. So fast. I must have struck a nerve.

Screw him. I'd deal with him when I was ready.

———————

Norman Bates stared right through me. His face filled the screen, the image of a skull superimposed on him. I shuddered. Creepy.

The lights came up and the bell rang. "Okay, folks," Mrs. Carney said. "I want your two-page reflection papers on *Psycho* by Friday. Or *Mother* will be very upset."

Everyone laughed as they filed out of the room. Ricky tapped me on the shoulder. "Good luck," he said, nodding at Carney. We bumped fists and I hung back, waiting to get Carney alone.

"Carmen," she said once the classroom was empty, "please don't tell me Norman Bates has been giving you nightmares."

"No, Mrs. Carney, I was just . . ." I stopped. "Do you like me, Mrs. Carney?"

She sat down on the corner of her desk. "I can't think of anyone I dislike. Have I done something to make you think . . . ?"

"Oh, no," I said quickly. "No, just the opposite. I think you're the only teacher at Southside who treats me like a human being."

She frowned. "I'm really sorry to hear that. I hope it's not true, but I'm sure that must be how it seems. Is it something you wanted to talk about?"

I shook my head. "No, not really. I just . . ." I got out the petition. "I'm trying to start a GSA. I need to get three faculty members to sign but . . . well, teachers aren't exactly beating down my door. Vice Principal Winston says it's because I don't follow through."

Mrs. Carney looked over the petition. "I haven't had you in class long enough to know if that's true. You seem like a great student. You ask good questions, you participate in discussion. But, to be honest, I've heard that about you from other teachers."

I groaned. "Teachers *talk* about me?" Great. I really was doomed.

She smiled. "Teachers talk about *all* the students. You're not being singled out. I don't get the impression that people dislike you. But they think you're capable of more than you achieve. Getting this GSA started could show everyone they're wrong."

"But that's the problem," I said. "I *could* prove that I can follow through. This GSA means a lot to me. I think it would really help people, and I'd work hard to keep it running. But I need a chance first. Is there any way you'd consider signing this?"

Mrs. Carney tilted her head as she thought. "You know, you still need to get thirty students to sign this."

I waved my hand. "Oh, that's not a problem."

She seemed impressed. "Really?"

I shrugged. "Not to brag, but I have a lot of friends. I'm not über-popular, like Jessie Reed, but I fit in with lots of different groups. Thirty signatures isn't a problem. It's just those three."

She pursed her lips and handed the petition back to me. "I'll tell you what: can you come here tomorrow morning before the first bell rings? I might have a solution to your problem."

I tried not to look devastated that she hadn't signed it. I just took the petition back and signed. "Sure thing," I said. "I'll be here first thing in the morning."

As I headed for my locker, I wondered what kind of solution Mrs. Carney had in mind. Because if she couldn't deliver those three faculty signatures, the GSA was over before it had even begun.

CHAPTER 9

SCOTT

My phone started playing "Yellow Rose of Texas." Cory's ringtone. I tapped a button and sent it to voicemail. It was the fifth time she'd tried calling since our fight. I so wasn't ready to talk to her yet.

I sat at my laptop in my bedroom, trying to ignore the petition next to me that still only had my signature on it. I was ready to give up completely. I almost went to Mr. Winston to ask permission to recruit during the other lunch periods, but then I thought about Shelly and Maggie. Yeah, I was a jerk to them. I used to be a real jerk to a lot of people. I stopped all that when Jamie came out to me. I couldn't get over how brave he'd been. And he was right: if I wasn't going to tease him about being gay, I couldn't lay into anyone else either.

But just because I'd quit being a jerk didn't mean that people quit hating me for what I'd done. How many people hated me as much as Shelly and Maggie? Was it even worth it to figure out?

My phone buzzed, and I was just about to pick it up and tell Cory off when I realized the phone wasn't playing "Yellow Rose of Texas." I checked the screen. It was Mr. Ballard.

"Hey, Mr. Ballard," I said.

"Hi, Scott. How are you?"

"Well . . . you know."

"Yeah. Yeah, I know. Listen, the police are still looking into whoever was harassing Jamie. Did he ever say anything to you?"

"No," I said quickly. "You gotta know,

Mr. Ballard, that if I knew *anybody* was giving Jamie a hard time—"

"I understand. I didn't mean to say you weren't a good friend to Jamie. I just thought maybe he said something to you. Even if you didn't realize he was trying to tell you something. Anything that might be able to help the police . . . ?"

I thought about it. The week before he died, Jamie had been all smiles. He couldn't stop talking about this guy he met on-line who went to Northside High. They were talking about meeting in person to get some coffee. I'd never seen him happier.

Then, the day before he killed himself, we hung out at the mall, talking about senior year. He hardly cracked a smile all night. He didn't mention the Northside guy at all. When I asked him what was wrong, he said he was worried about passing all his classes and getting into a good school. It didn't make sense. Jamie was a great student. I just thought he was nervous about senior year. But I never got to ask him about it more because the next day he was dead.

"I can't think of anything, Mr. Ballard. But if I do, I'll let you know."

Mr. Ballard thanked me and hung up. I turned back to my laptop. Mr. Ballard had given Jamie's cell phone to the cops to see if they could figure out who'd been harassing him. I remember him saying that the jerk who was harassing him had done it on-line too. Which meant he probably left a trail . . .

I pulled up Jamie's Twitter stream. A lot of it was flirting with @NHSDramaGuy. I assumed that was the Northside guy he liked. But as I scrolled through the stream, I started finding other tweets.

@HoustonJamie if u killed yourself no one would care

@HoustonJamie houstons dirty enough without fags like you messing things up

@HoustonJamie really just die already cant stand seeing your face in the halls

They were all from somebody named VictorEE. I didn't know anybody named Victor. I looked through last year's yearbook for the initials E. E. Nothing.

Cant stand seeing your face in the halls.

That could only mean one thing. Whoever it was went to Southside.

I clicked on VictorEE's profile to see if I could figure out who they were. They didn't list their real name, of course. Most of their tweets were talk about the Cowboys and the Oilers. When VictorEE wasn't talking sports, he—it had to be a he—was mocking people. He told someone named @RainbowTexan they should drink acid. He told @TerryHarlow that AIDS was God's vengeance.

Most recently, VictorEE was hating on just one person. His five latest tweets had all been aimed at @CMendoza. I clicked on CMendoza's profile and saw the photo of a girl I recognized.

Carmen Mendoza. I kind of knew who she was. Everyone knew she was a lesbian. She lived in River Oaks, the rich part of town, but you'd never know it by how she dressed. Unlike most rich girls, who flaunted what they had, Carmen never made it a thing. That's why a lot of people liked her.

According to her feed, she was giving back to VictorEE just as good as she was getting. She seemed to enjoy making him angry. But the more she stuck it to him, the more violent his tweets got. I hoped she knew enough to watch her back.

That settled it for me. I *had* to talk to Mr. Winston about recruiting in other lunch periods. So people hated me. I'd have to find a way around that. Southside *needed* a GSA to deal with just the sort of thing that was happening to Carmen Mendoza. I couldn't stop now.

— — — — —

I got to school early, hoping to catch Mr. Winston. Convincing him to let me visit all the lunch periods wouldn't be too hard. My grades were perfect. I'd only be missing English—which I was acing—and a study hall.

But as I walked through the doors, I heard an overhead announcement.

"Scott King, please report to Mrs. Carney in Room 318. Scott King to room 318."

Mrs. Carney? I was still a bit sore about the advice she'd given me. Talking to the football team had ended with the team ignoring me and me breaking up with my girlfriend.

When I got to Room 318, she invited me in and closed the door. Sitting at a table across from her desk was the girl I'd seen last night on Twitter: Carmen Mendoza. She didn't look thrilled to see me.

"Sit down, Scott," Mrs. Carney said. "I think the two of you need to talk."

CHAPTER 10

CARMEN

"**S**trangers on a Train."

Mrs. Carney sat at her desk, waiting for us to respond to the weird thing she'd just said.

"Excuse me?" I asked.

"It's a Hitchcock movie," Scott said. "We watched it last year in Media Studies."

I frowned. The last thing I needed was Scott King lecturing me on movie history.

Why was he even here? Mrs. Carney said she wanted to help me get signatures for the petition. There was no way I could think of where that solution involved Scott "Golden Boy" King.

Mrs. Carney nodded. "Glad you remember it. Tell Carmen what it's about."

Scott looked at me like he had no idea why she was asking this. "Well, it's about these two guys who meet on a train. One is a tennis player who hates his wife because she won't divorce him. The other is this rich guy, or at least he would be rich if his dad gave him the family money. These two guys talk about the people they hate, and the rich guy says the easiest way to solve their problems would be to kill them.

"But they can't just *do* it. They've each got a motive. The police would figure it out quick and arrest them. So, the rich guy suggests they swap murders. 'Crisscross,' he called it. The rich guy would kill the tennis player's wife, and the tennis player would kill the rich guy's dad. No one would suspect anything."

I turned to Carney. "What does this have to do with anything? You said you'd help me get the signatures I needed for the GSA petition."

Scott held up his hand. "Wait a minute. What GSA petition? You mean *my* GSA petition."

I whirled on him. "No, I mean *my* GSA petition. I'm trying to start a *real* GSA."

Scott's brow furrowed. "And you think my GSA isn't real?"

"Okay, both of you, stand down," Mrs. Carney said. "This isn't about real or fake GSAs. You both have the same goal. But, from what I understand, you're having trouble reaching it. Am I right?"

I looked down at my desk. Out of the corner of my eye, I saw Scott doing the same. We were both quiet for a long time.

"I can't get any teachers to sign," I said finally. "Just three lousy names is all I need, and I can't get them."

Scott laughed. "You're joking, right? Getting teachers to sign on is the easy part.

I can think of six who'd be willing. Just try finding thirty students in this school who give a damn about starting a Gay–Straight Alliance. They're either afraid of being labeled queer, or they're too homophobic to care."

"Well," I said, "you obviously haven't been talking to the right students, because I could fill that petition with signatures, but they're useless without teachers . . ."

Right about then, both Scott and I noticed that Mrs. Carney was leaning back and beaming, looking like the cat that swallowed the canary, as my mom would say.

"Crisscross," she said simply. "Carmen, you fit in a lot of different cliques. People respect you. You ask them to sign, and they'll sign. Scott, Carmen's right. All the signatures in the world won't do any good if you can't get three faculty members to sign. There's not a teacher in this school who doesn't use you as an example of a good student. They'll listen to you."

I looked over at Scott, who'd gone red with embarrassment. Chances are, I was looking the same way too. It was an obvious solution.

I didn't exactly like the idea of working with this guy. Everyone knew what a self-involved jerk he was. But Mrs. Carney was right. The faculty loved him. I didn't trust him not to abandon the GSA once it got going, but if he could get us there, it didn't matter. Starting the GSA was the only thing that mattered.

Scott pulled out his petition. At the bottom, where it said NAME OF STUDENT ORGANZIER, he'd already filled in his name. With a black pen, he added my name next to his, then handed me the petition.

"Unless you want your name on there first?" he asked. I almost thought he was being nice.

"That's okay," I said. "Winston will take it more seriously if he sees your name first."

Scott laughed. "Can't wait to see the look on his face when he sees *both* our names on this."

Without even wanting to, I broke into a smile. Maybe *that* would be the best thing to come out of this: watching Winston's face explode.

Mrs. Carney looked at the clock. "First period starts soon. You should get heading to class."

"Uh, not so fast," I said, putting my hands on my hips. "You brought us together. That means you *must* support the idea of a GSA, right?"

Scott grinned and slid our petition over to her. "Someone's got to set a good example for the other teachers, Mrs. Carney. We sure could use a faculty advisor."

Mrs. Carney reached into her desk and pulled out a pen. "I thought you'd never ask."

And as the first bell of the day rang, she signed her name in big, bright, beautiful red ink at the very top of the petition. The door opened, and students started pouring in.

Mrs. Carney greeted them quickly, then turned back to us. "You've got a lot of work to do, you two. I'll be very disappointed if my name is the only one on the top of that petition by the end of the day."

Scott and I stepped out into the hall. He held up the petition. "I can get the next two signatures easy. Meet me at my locker— number twenty-seven—before fourth period and I'll pass it off to you."

I nodded. If *anyone* during my lunch period thought they were leaving the cafeteria without signing, they were in for a huge surprise. I quickly added my name to his on the petition.

"Try not to let the teachers see my name before you ask them to sign," I said. "They might change their minds."

He laughed. "Are you kidding? With your name on here, all I have to do is threaten them that if they don't sign, you'll take up every minute of class time arguing with them. They'll sign in a second."

Scott took the petition and wove through the hall.

All I have to do is threaten them that if they don't sign, you'll take up every minute of class time arguing with them.

Now why hadn't *I* thought of that?

CHAPTER 11

SCOTT

Mr. Rosencranz studied the petition carefully, reading it over and over and not saying a word. First period AP History had just let out. The room was almost completely empty, and the next class would be arriving shortly. Which meant I wouldn't have a lot of time to get to my next class if he didn't sign soon.

"I'm not asking you to be the advisor," I said, trying to speed him up. "See? Mrs.

Carney signed there, saying she'd do that. All I need is two more signatures from faculty saying they think a GSA would be a good idea. I know you must have seen your share of bullying in the halls, Mr. Rosencranz. I'm sure you don't want to be condemned to repeat that."

As a lover of history, there was a quote Mr. Rosencranz was always fond of: *Those who cannot remember the past are condemned to repeat it.*

He looked up at me over the rims of his glasses. "Trying to use my own quotations against me, Mr. King?" A hint of a smile told me he was more proud I remembered the quote than angry I was playing him.

But the smile disappeared as he held up the petition. "I assume this has something to do with Jamie Ballard."

"Yes, sir."

"Yes. I remember the two of you sitting in the back of my room during junior year, laughing as we talked about the Vietnam War."

"Sorry, sir."

Mr. Rosencranz sighed. "I really admire what you're doing here. But I feel compelled to warn you that you may not know what you're getting into. There is a very strong conservative element in this school. You may not see it every day, but it's there. Usually working behind the scenes. There are those who won't appreciate you trying to start this group. Some might even try to stop it."

I just couldn't understand that. Why try to stop a group that only wanted to help? Creating a place for queer students to feel safe was a *good* thing. Why couldn't people see that?

"Maybe, sir, but I have to try," I said. "For Jamie."

He nodded, got out his pen, and signed his name next to Mrs. Carney's. "If anyone can do it, Mr. King, it's you. Oh, and Ms. Mendoza. She's quite the firebrand, isn't she?"

I smiled. "I'll tell her you said so, sir. I'm sure she'll be happy to hear it." The class was nearly full. I'd be late if I didn't hustle. "Thanks!"

I bolted from the room to find Cory leaning against the wall nearby.

"Hey," she said, waving.

"Hey," I said. "Look, I gotta get to class."

"Can I walk with you?" she asked.

"As long as you're going my way," I said and moved down the hall.

Cory fell into step next to me. "I'm sorry things ended the way they did, Scott. I'm hoping we can still be friends."

My heart beat hard in my chest. If I told her no, was I as guilty of intolerance as she was? "I guess," I said. "Maybe."

Cory hugged herself with her arms, which was not a good sign. She only did that when she was really nervous.

"Okay, good," she said. "So, as a friend, I need to tell you. You really need to quit trying to make this GSA happen."

I growled. "I'm not quitting, Cory. And a *friend* wouldn't try to talk me out of it. A *friend* would support me."

"My mama's not happy about this, Scott."

I stopped dead in my tracks. Cory's mom, Sheila Walton, was well-known. She was a prominent member of the local Baptist church and had spearheaded several attempts to get books banned from the school. Some of them even succeeded. She was someone you didn't make mad. She could be sweet as pie one minute and your worst nightmare the next.

"You told your mama?" I asked.

She nodded. "I was really worried about you. Honest, I was. She said she won't let the school sanction sodomy."

"The school's not sanctioning sodomy, for crying out loud!"

"If the GSA gets approved, they can get school money. School money is tax money. And she doesn't want her tax money spent to glorify sin."

I really wanted to let her have it with both barrels. Just yell at her until I was hoarse about what a horrible bigot she and her mama were. But I didn't have time. Besides, as long as Carmen and I did our jobs and got the petition signed, there was nothing Mrs. Walton could do to stop us.

"Anything else?" I asked her.

Cory hugged herself even tighter. "I didn't want you to hear it from anybody else. I'm seeing somebody new."

I felt my ears flush. I knew that I had broken us up, but it still stung to know she'd moved on so fast. Her phone chirped. She took it out and smiled.

"He's always texting me cute little things," she said. "You may be mad at me, Scott, but I do want to be friends, okay? No matter what happens."

I looked over her shoulder at the text message:

SEE U 2 NIGHT? V.

I grunted. "Who's V?"

"It's just his nickname," Cory said with a giggle. "He uses it online. Short for VictorEE."

I snatched the phone away and checked the inbox.

VictorEE was Jon Renquist.

CHAPTER 12

CARMEN

"**A**ll right, everybody! Forks down, eyes up, and *listen!*"

I stood on a table in the middle of the cafeteria, my algebra homework rolled up into a megaphone. Two years of drama and this lesbian could *project*. Instantly, everyone quieted down. All eyes fell on me.

"Show of hands: how many people here knew Jamie Ballard?"

I counted about twelve hands. I knew it wasn't true, but I went with it.

"For those of you who didn't know him, Jamie went to this school. He was your classmate. Recently, he killed himself. You see, Jamie was gay. And some people had a problem with that, and they wouldn't let him forget it.

"And I bet some of you know what that's like. I bet *a lot* of you know what it's like to be shoved into a wall or called gay, whether it's true or not. And I've got a feeling you'd like it to stop. Well, I'm here to tell you *it can stop!*"

"Do it, Carmen!" Somebody yelled. Applause broke out. People whooped.

I held up the petition. "Southside High needs a Gay–Straight Alliance. You don't have to be gay to join. You just have to care. You have to want to see everyone treated fairly. And the only way to get this to happen is to speak up. To put your name down on this piece of paper and tell the administration that you want to see the bullying end."

A handful of students had already gathered near my table, pens in hand. I slipped the petition down to Ricky, who started lining people up for signing. I pulled my fake megaphone closer and kept at it.

"Signing this doesn't mean joining. It could mean that you're tired of staying silent. It could mean that you won't stand by anymore when you see someone getting the crap beat out of them because somebody else *thinks* that person is gay. Or it could mean that you *do* want to join and work to make Southside safe for everybody: queer, straight, or whatever."

The signing line snaked around the nearest tables. People were banging their trays on the tables in support. The aides who monitored the lunch room—retirees with as much authority as a wet mop—were standing below, motioning me to get down. But I was on a roll.

"I won't lie to you. Some people don't want us to start this group. Some people are happy to keep things the way they are. These people are *cowards*."

The crowd grumbled their approval. Ricky gave me the thumbs-up. "We've got fifty signatures already. Keep going."

"Yeah, I said it. *Cowards.* They're the ones who want to keep the power right where it is: with them. They hide behind fake names online, too scared to admit who they really are."

I scanned the room. There were three lunch periods, which meant I had a one in three shot of VictorEE being here. I figured if I made him mad enough . . .

"Well, I'll tell you who they really are. You can't miss them. *They've got the tiniest dicks in four counties!*"

A roar of laughter rippled through the students. I held up my arms, basking in their attention.

Splat!

My head snapped to the side as something hot and wet pelted the side of my face. My vision blurred. As soon as I could see, I looked down to see a slab of meatloaf on the floor. When I turned, I found Jon Renquist standing on the table next to me, murder in his eyes. He clutched another piece of meatloaf in his left hand.

"What do you know about dicks, you ugly dyke?" Ren shouted. He pitched the meatloaf at me, but this time I ducked.

I pointed my megaphone at him. "It's like art: I know one when I see one. And guess where I'm looking right now..."

Was this really VictorEE? It totally made sense. Somehow, I found it disappointing. It was almost too obvious. Too cliché. But then, I wasn't about to give Ren points for original thinking.

When everyone went "oooh," the veins in Ren's neck bulged with rage. "The only reason she's a lesbian is because she hasn't been with a real man."

I raised an eyebrow at him. "I'm game. Let me know as soon as you see one, Renquist."

Ren leaped off the table and charged. The aides were flung aside as the linebacker bore down on me. I braced myself, waiting to get knocked to the ground.

But a blur swept past me and tackled Ren just before he reached the table. In an instant everyone was out of their seats and standing in a circle, chanting, "Fight! Fight!"

I moved to the end of the long table and found Ren wrestling on the ground with Scott

King. Ren was bigger, but he sucked at ground fighting. In no time, Scott was on top, raining punch after punch down.

Suddenly, Ren jerked his knee up and slammed Scott in the back. A second later the tables were turned, with Ren pinning Scott's arms to the ground with his knees and landing blow after blow in Scott's stomach.

I tossed my algebra homework aside and jumped, crashing into Ren. All three of us tumbled around in the middle of the circle while the other students cheered us on. I grabbed a handful of Ren's hair and was about to punch him in the ear when a pair of powerful hands yanked me away. I looked up to find Mr. Winston pulling me back. Two other male teachers broke through the circle and separated Ren and Scott.

"It was Ren, Mr. Winston," Scott said, his lower lip already growing fat. "He was bullying Jamie. And he's been bullying Carmen online too."

"We'll sort that out later," Winston said. "Right now, to the office. All three of you."

CHAPTER 13

SCOTT

I sat in the mall food court at the same table where Jamie and I had spent many summers. He'd look for hot guys, and I'd look for hot girls, and we'd question each other's taste. It usually ended with one of us in a headlock. I'd have given anything to do that with him again.

It was the middle of the second day of the three-day suspension I got for fighting. Mom and Dad weren't exactly happy, but when I explained the whole story, they let me off with a warning. Said I wasn't to fight anymore.

But I had a feeling that a different kind of fight was coming. I thought about what Cory said about the GSA and what Mr. Rosencranz said about people getting upset. We were going to make a lot of people angry.

"Is this seat taken?"

I looked up to find Carmen with a tray from Sbarro. I pulled a chair out for her, and she sat.

"Enjoying your vacation?" she asked.

I squinted at her with the eye that had nearly swollen shut. "Yeah. It's been a blast."

"A shiner works on you," she said. "Very manly."

I grunted. "I'll keep that in mind."

"Hey, listen, thanks for, you know, tackling Ren. He's gotta have at least thirty pounds on you."

"We took him on together. But I think the first order of business for the GSA is to arrange a self-defense course. We're not very good at it."

She chuckled and gnawed on her pizza. We were quiet for a long time.

"Carmen?"

"Yeah?"

"You know before, when I said I couldn't get people to sign because they were afraid of being labeled queer or they were homophobic? It was only part true. Most people wouldn't sign because I was a jerk."

"I kind of figured."

"Thanks for rubbing it in."

"No problem."

I shook my head. "I gave people crap for a long time. I never saw it as bullying. I kept thinking, 'I'm not beating anybody up. Bullying is when you beat people up.' Guess I got it wrong."

She offered me a breadstick. I grabbed one and dipped it in the marinara. "Some people can go their whole lives and not realize what a dirtbag they are. At least you figured it out."

"No. Jamie figured it out. He told me what a knob I was being."

"Right. And you listened, you changed, and now you're trying to do the right thing. He'd be proud of you."

I choked up, thinking about it. Looking back, I guess I always wanted Jamie to be proud of me. At least as proud as I was of him. He was the bravest guy I knew.

"Did you know Jamie?" I asked.

She nodded. "A little. We had chemistry together last year. His lab table was kitty-corner from mine. I remember he used to cackle like a mad scientist every time he poured one beaker into another: *Bwah-hah-ha!*"

I laughed. "Yep. That's Jamie."

Carmen slurped on her soda. "So, the other day, you told Winston that Ren had been harassing me online. How'd you know about that?"

I told her about reading Jamie's Twitter stream and seeing how Ren had been bugging both Jamie and her. "He's a complete psycho. That's why I went looking for you in the cafeteria as soon as I found out. I think he really would have hurt you."

She shrugged. "Maybe. Doesn't matter now. He may have gotten the same three-day suspension that we got, but I think it'll be a while before we see him back in school."

"Why's that?"

"He put a death threat in my locker, and I showed it to the police."

"You're kidding!"

"Nope. I sat on it for a long time, thinking I'd deal with it myself. The last thing I wanted was to give some jerk the satisfaction of knowing he got under my skin. But when we were getting chewed out by Winston, I realized that the only way to stop the bullying is to expose it. If we hide it, we're giving the bullies permission to keep on doing it."

I swallowed hard. I knew just what she meant. That's why I'd never let up on Maggie. I knew nobody knew, so I figured it was okay to keep going. I was such a jerk.

"Anyway," she said, "Ren's eighteen, so they're pressing charges. He could get expelled."

It would suck to get expelled senior year. But he had it coming. "I'm glad you didn't get hurt."

"So," she said quickly, like she was trying to change the subject. "We've got a major decision to make."

"What's that?"

"Who is going to be president, and who is going to be vice president of the GSA? I'll arm wrestle you for it."

I leaned away in mock fear. "I've seen you in a fight. You'd rip my arm off. I'm happy to be vice president."

"Or," she said with a smile, "we could be co-presidents. It's a tough job. It'd be good to have somebody to help shoulder the load."

I nodded. "Co-president? I could deal with that."

She held out her hand, and we shook. "You know," she said, "we had all those people sign the petition. It's no guarantee they're all gonna join the GSA."

"School charter says any club has to have a minimum of three members. We got you, me, and your friend Ricky. The important thing is that Winston doesn't have any excuse not to sign off on the club."

Carmen *hmphed* and rattled the ice around in her cup. "I'll believe it when I see it . . ."

CHAPTER 14

CARMEN

First day back from our suspension, before classes started, Scott and I went to Mr. Winston with our petition.

"As you can see," I said, trying hard not to sound as smug as Winston usually looked, "we got one hundred student signatures. We could have gotten more, but we ran out of room. Maybe the petitions need to be bigger."

"And after three teachers signed, I got

verbal promises from six others that they support the creation of a GSA at Southside as well," Scott said. "And Mr. Rosencranz offered to be the co-advisor with Mrs. Carney."

"There's a lot of support for this, Mr. Winston," I said. "All we need is for you to sign at the bottom to make it official."

Winston eyed the petition. "So, who will be running this . . . alliance?"

Scott and I looked at each other. "Well, we want to do it together," I said. "A straight boy, a queer girl . . . That's what the GSA is all about."

Winston sighed, then rifled through his desk, looking for a pen. "If you read the charters, you know that all new organizations go through a ninety-day probation period. At the end of that time, you need to turn in a list of elected officers, minutes for your first three meetings, and detailed plans on how to use the money you'll be allotted as a school-sanctioned club."

I shot a look at Scott. This was really happening!

We heard a knock behind us and turned to

find Principal Rice standing in the doorway. "Sorry to interrupt, Mr. Winston," she said. "Could I have a word?"

Winston nodded, and the pair went into the hallway. We watched as she spoke quickly to Winston, who scowled and nodded. They both kept sneaking looks our way.

"This can't be good," Scott said.

I shook my head. "We followed the rules. We did everything by the book. They can't stop us now."

Rice gave Winston a pat on the back, waved at us, and left. Winston trudged back into his office, closing the door so the three of us could have privacy.

"Something's come up," he said. I couldn't tell if he was happy or upset. I think he was trying hard not to be either. "The GSA is on hold. Indefinitely."

Scott was the first out of his seat. "Why?"

"The school board had an emergency meeting last night. A concerned parent group got wind of plans for the alliance and prompted the board to put a stop to it."

"They can't do that!" My hands were shaking I was so mad. All I could think about was calling my parents and having them go all legal on the school board.

Winston, for just a second, looked somewhat sympathetic. "They *have* done that. They feel homosexuality is a hot-button issue right now. They've implemented a 'neutrality' policy. Teachers are not to discuss it. The school is to take no side on the issue. And because starting a Gay–Straight Alliance could be seen as endorsing the 'hot-button issue,' we're not allowed to start one. I'm sorry."

I stood there, hardly able to believe any of this. Scott was stonefaced, but I got the idea he was holding a lot in. He couldn't take his eyes off the petition. We'd worked so hard on it. Now it was all for nothing.

"Mr. Winston," Scott said quietly, "could you keep that on file? Just in case the school board changes its mind."

Winston grimaced. "I can do that, Mr. King. But these things don't resolve themselves overnight. I'm sure it won't be long before lawyers are involved . . ." He snuck a furtive glance my way. "And once this becomes a legal matter, it might not get decided until long after the two of you have graduated. What I'm saying is: don't get your hopes up."

But, like he said he'd do, he opened a drawer and slid the petition into a file.

We thanked him and left the office. The warning bell rang, telling everyone it was time to get to first period.

"Cory . . ." Scott muttered under his breath.

"What was that?"

"Cory Walton. I bet her mama's behind this. She pretty much told me this would happen. I didn't believe her."

"You couldn't have known she'd take it this far."

Scott's shoulders slumped. "We were so close . . ."

"Hey," I said, nudging him. "You're talking like it's over. Sweetie, this was just the first battle. I'm not about to quit the war. And neither are you. Right?"

For a second, I thought he was gonna throw in the towel. His eyes got all dark, and he couldn't stop staring at the floor. Then, somewhere down the hall, we heard somebody say, "Hey, watch it, Jones! You faggot!" People laughed. To them, it was just another insult.

But it wasn't. Suddenly, it was like somebody lit a fire under him. Scott lifted his head and stuck out his jaw.

"For Jamie?" he asked, holding out his arm.

I hooked my elbow with his and looked him square in the eye.

"For *everyone*."

About the Author

Gabriel Goodman is a writer living in St. Paul, Minnesota.

SOUTHSIDE HIGH

ARE YOU A SURVIVOR?

The Alliance

Bad Deal

Beaten

Benito Runs

Dance Team

Deadly Drive

The Fight

Full Impact

Overexposed

Plan B

Recruited

Shattered Star

check out all the books in the

SURVIVING SOUTH SIDE

collection